NEW BABY

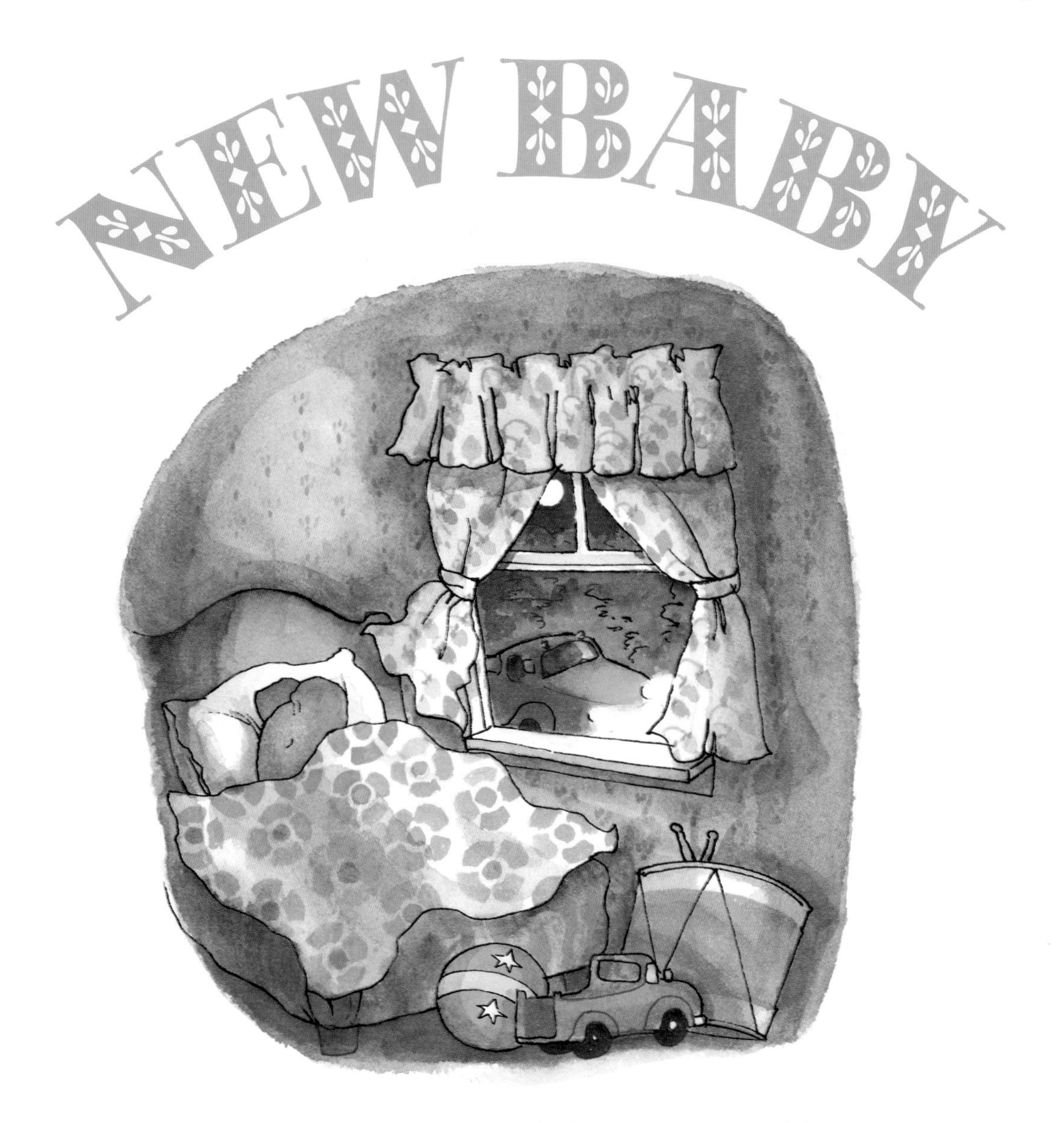

Emily Arnold McCully

HARPER & ROW, PUBLISHERS

New Baby

10 9 8 7 6 5 4 3 2 1
First Edition

Library of Congress Cataloging-in-Publication Data
McCully, Emily Arnold.
New baby.

Summary: The youngest mouse in a large family discovers excitement and frustration when a new baby arrives.
[1. Mice—Fiction. 2. Babies—Fiction. 3. Family life—Fiction. 4. Stories without words]
I. Title.
PZ7.M478415Ne 1988 [E] 87-45294
ISBN 0-06-024130-6
ISBN 0-06-024131-4 (lib. bdg.)

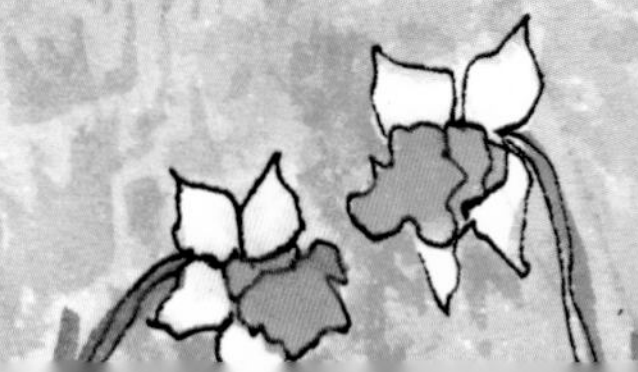